A HUSBAND FOR CHRISTMAS
A Mistletoe Kisses Romance

EM TATE

Copyright © 2024 by Em Tate

All rights reserved.

No part of this book may be reproduced in any form or by any electronic or mechanical means, including information storage and retrieval systems, without written permission from the author, except for the use of brief quotations in a book review.

For my Family at Christmas

Chapter 1

Lily

The first thing I notice when I wake up is the pounding in my head, like a tiny marching band has decided to rehearse inside my skull. The second thing I notice is that I'm not alone.

There's a guy. In bed. Next to me.

I jolt upright, which is a terrible decision. The room spins like I'm on some amusement park ride that I never asked to be on, and I immediately regret everything that's led me, the Parker family screw-up, to this moment. Everything.

"What the—?" I mutter, glancing down at myself. My dress is still on. A little wrinkled, but on. I look over at the guy again—he's fully clothed too. Suit jacket, tie... like he just passed out after a long night of bad decisions.

Okay, maybe nothing catastrophic happened. At least not in that sense.

I relax just a smidge—until my eyes land on something shiny on my left hand. Something very... ring-shaped.

Oh no. *Oh no no no no.*

I hold my hand up to the light like it's on fire, squinting at the simple gold band circling my ring finger.

No. Way.

"Please tell me this is a prank," I whisper to no one in particular, praying for hidden cameras or a very elaborate dream.

At that moment, the guy stirs next to me, groaning. Slowly, he sits up, his large callous hand rubbing his face. He's disheveled, his brown, thick hair sticking up in every possible direction like he's just walked out of a wind tunnel. He blinks his dark, red-rimmed eyes at me blearily.

"Good morning... wife."

Wife?!

I stare at him, wide-eyed. "Did you just call me 'wife'?"

He glances down at his own hand, and—oh, perfect—there's a matching ring on his finger. "Looks like it," he says, a hint of amusement in his voice, as if this is some kind of joke.

I gape at him, waiting for my brain to catch up. "Okay, um, first of all, who are you?"

The corner of his mouth lifts in a lazy grin, like this is the most normal situation in the world. "I'm Cole. And you're Lily. Unless you've changed your name since last night, in which case, this marriage is off to a rocky start."

"Cole." I test it out, and it doesn't even sound real. "Well, Cole, care to explain why I'm wearing a wedding ring? On my ring finger?"

He stretches his arms above his head, clearly in no rush to address my impending panic attack. "I'm gonna go out on a limb and say it's because we got married."

"Married? As in, legally bound by the laws of Nevada?" I point at the ring like it's a ticking bomb. "How?!"

"Well, usually, it involves vows, a quick visit to a chapel, and—"

"I know how marriage works!" I cut him off, feeling my pulse quicken. "I just don't remember the part where I agreed to any of it!"

Cole shrugs, annoyingly calm for someone who just woke up to find himself with a brand-new wife. "After we connected at the casino bar, you had a grand plan to bring me home to distract your family over the holidays. You said something about not being perfect and tired of playing a supporting actress role to your sister. You might've been a little tipsy."

"Oh, you think?" I laugh, but it's more of a manic, what-the-heck-is-happening kind of laugh. "Why would you even agree to a drunk stranger's plan? We need to fix this. Like, immediately."

"I mean, I'm not doing anything for the holidays and you are cute. I mean, we could just let this ride for a bit. See how your grand holiday plan goes."

I gape at him again. "See how it goes? Are you out of your mind?"

Cole tilts his head, considering. "Possibly. But think about it—it's the holidays. You're going home to see your family, right? They are waiting for you to screw up and your sister is waiting to flaunt her perfect family to you—or at least that's what I gathered from you last night, right?"

"Yeah… so?"

"So, what's a better way to spread Christmas cheer and change your usual holiday than bringing home your brand-new husband?"

I blink at him. "Are you serious right now?"

He grins. "Well, I already have the ring, so why not?"

Oh, I can think of so many reasons why not.

"We don't even know each other," I sputter. "You could be a serial killer!"

Cole raises an eyebrow. "Do serial killers usually wear three-thousand dollar suits?"

"You'd make an excellent disguised serial killer. Charming, well-dressed, casually murdering people in between dinner parties."

He chuckles, leaning back against the headboard like we're discussing the weather. "I promise, no serial killing. Scout's honor."

"Convenient that I don't have time to fact-check that."

Cole reaches for his phone and glances at the time. "So… what's the plan, Lily? You want a quick annulment, or are we gonna make this the Christmas of a lifetime?"

I groan, dropping my head into my hands. This cannot be my life right now. "I can't bring you home. My family will freak out."

"Oh, come on. What's the worst that could happen? They'll probably love me."

I give him a flat look. "Or they'll think I've lost my mind. Which, to be fair, isn't entirely wrong."

Cole's eyes twinkle, clearly enjoying every second of this chaos. "Look, we'll just go home, explain the situation, and get it annulled after the holidays. Easy peasy."

I stare at him, trying to figure out why he's so calm about all of this. I mean, we literally accidentally got married, and now he's acting like it's just a fun adventure.

"Besides," he adds, "it might be fun. You know, playing house for a bit."

"Playing house," I repeat, deadpan.

He flashes me a grin that's infuriatingly charming. "Could be worse, right?"

I sigh, long and hard. "I'm going to regret this, aren't I?"

Cole shrugs. "Only one way to find out, Mrs. … uh, what's your last name?"

"Parker. Lily Parker."

"Well, Lily Parker, meet Cole Rivers. Your brand-new husband. For the next few weeks, anyway."

I look at this ruggedly handsome man, the type I usually fall for but who never seem to notice me. The man I somehow ended up accidentally married to, and I feel a strange mix of exasperation and something that feels suspiciously like excitement.

Maybe, just maybe, this isn't the worst thing that could've happened.

But it's probably still pretty close.

Chapter 2

Lily

I stare at Cole Rivers—my husband, apparently—and try to piece together the events of last night like a puzzle that's missing half its pieces.

But the truth is, I remember absolutely nothing. Nada. Zilch. My mind is a blank slate, like someone took an eraser to the entire night. All I know is that at some point, between a glass of wine and what should've been a quiet night of wallowing in my holiday dread, I ended up with a ring on my finger and a husband. A husband.

It doesn't make sense. None of this makes sense.

"You're sure we got married?" I ask for what must be the third time, peeking at the simple gold band on my finger like it's going to start glowing and offer some magical explanation.

Cole leans back against the headboard, hands resting casually behind his head, looking far too comfortable for a man who's just as legally confused as I am. "Yep. Chapel, vows, the whole deal. Very heartfelt."

"Heartfelt," I repeat, incredulous. "And you're not freaking out? At all?"

He flashes me that same lazy grin. "Not really. You seemed pretty into it."

"I—" I stop myself. I seemed into it? This just gets better and better. "Okay, we have to rewind. Because I don't remember any of this. Like, at all."

"Well, I did mention you were a little out of it."

"Out of it?" My brain scrambles to make sense of that. "I had one glass of wine."

"That's true," he agrees. "But you did say something about meds."

I freeze. Oh.

Right. The new migraine medication I'd started last week. My doctor did warn me that mixing alcohol with it might cause... unexpected side effects. But I hadn't really paid attention because, I don't know, I figured one glass of wine wasn't going to kill me.

Apparently, it didn't kill me. Just married me off instead.

I slump back against the pillows, groaning. "This is a nightmare. I'm literally living in a cautionary tale. Don't mix medication with alcohol, or you might wake up married to a complete stranger."

Cole chuckles, completely unfazed. "Hey, I'm not that much of a stranger. We had a pretty decent conversation before things went... marital."

"Oh yeah?" I narrow my eyes at him, folding my arms over my chest. "What did we talk about?"

"Well..." He thinks for a moment, then ticks off on his fingers. "You told me about your sister, Jane—married, two kids, picture-perfect life—and how you were dreading going home for the holidays because you didn't want to be compared to her."

My stomach drops. "I said that?"

He nods. "You were having kind of a rough night."

A rough night? That doesn't even begin to cover it. Jane, with her magazine-spread-worthy life, her handsome husband, and two perfectly behaved children. Me, with my stressful job and zero romantic prospects, on the brink of another family gathering where I'd be the odd one out. I had been dreading it. The thought of sitting through another holiday season, smiling through gritted teeth as my mom fawned over Jane and her domestic bliss...

I can't even look at Cole. Instead, I stare at the ceiling, feeling the weight of that single glass of wine and all the stupid thoughts it had unleashed. I'd probably been thinking about how much easier life would be if I could just walk into my parents' house with a husband on my arm. Show everyone I wasn't the family disappointment, the perpetually single sister who doesn't measure up with Jane's fairytale existence.

I must've wished for a husband. And the universe, in all its terrible humor, decided to give me one.

"So, let me get this straight," I say slowly, pushing aside my shame. "I told you about my weird holiday inferiority complex, and then we just… got married?"

"Well, technically, you proposed." He smirks when I whip my head around to stare at him. "You don't remember? It was very romantic. You said something about how I'd make the perfect fake husband."

My jaw drops. "I proposed?!"

He shrugs. "Don't worry. I said yes."

"You said yes?!" I throw my hands up, completely horrified. "To a drunk, delirious stranger?"

Cole grins. "You seemed so sincere. How could I say no?"

I let out a frustrated groan. "This is not happening. I can't believe I'm married to some guy I don't even know. This is like… like the worst episode of a holiday romcom."

"Well, at least it's festive," he says, motioning to the garland hanging in the hotel room. "And, if you think about it, pretty convenient, too."

"Convenient?!" I practically shout. "In what universe is adding a fake marriage to my holiday stress convenient?"

"Think about it." Cole leans in a little, his blue eyes sparkling with amusement. "You were worried about going home for the holidays and being compared to your sister, right? Now, you get to bring your husband with you. Problem solved."

I stare at him, flabbergasted. "You think my solution to feeling inferior is to bring home a husband to my family Christmas?"

He shrugs. "It's got potential."

Potential? Potential to be a disaster, maybe.

"Look," I start, forcing my voice to sound calm even though I'm two seconds away from a full-blown panic attack. "I'm sure you're a nice guy, and this was clearly a mistake brought on by a bad reaction to medication, but we need to get this annulled. Like, today."

Cole holds up his hands in mock surrender. "You forgot to say Jason Momoa-like handsome. You had that in your vows, by the way. But it's Vegas, so it might take a couple of days. You know, bureaucracy and all."

I stare at him, trying to gauge if he's messing with me. "It's the holidays. How long are we talking?"

"Could be a week. Maybe two."

Two weeks.

Just long enough to get home, face the holiday horror, and somehow explain this. Perfect.

I groan again and fall back against the pillows. "This is a nightmare."

"Or," Cole says cheerfully, "this is an adventure."

I pull the covers over my head, moaning, "An adventure I didn't sign up for."

From underneath the covers, I hear him laugh softly. "Welcome to married life, Mrs. Rivers."

I peek out from under the blanket and glare at him. "Don't call me that."

But deep down, I know the universe is having a good laugh at my expense. Because somehow, some way, this total stranger is coming home with me for Christmas.

And I have absolutely no idea how to explain it to my family. I'm not telling them I married a complete stranger. My mother can assume that I've known Cole for a while. That we've been dating for months, and on a romantic whim we got married in Vegas. It's believable, right? *Right?*

Chapter 3

Cole

The snow-capped mountains of Colorado rise in the distance like some sort of picturesque holiday postcard as the SUV powers up the winding road toward Snowflake Village. It's exactly the kind of place people from the city would pay a small fortune to escape to during the holidays —quaint, tucked away, and relentlessly charming. Exactly the sort of place I never saw myself spending Christmas.

Except here I am, on my way to Lily's family cabin, married to a woman who has no idea what she's gotten herself into. Hell, I almost feel bad about it. Almost.

Lily sits in the passenger seat, her eyes hidden behind oversized sunglasses, trying to pretend she's not completely mortified about bringing me home. The tension between us is thick enough to cut with a knife, but I'm playing it cool. The charming husband, easygoing, supportive. Whatever it takes.

Because this is about more than our spontaneous Vegas wedding. This is about business. And business, especially in my world, doesn't have room for guilt.

I glance over at her as we drive. She's biting her lip, fingers tapping nervously against her leg. She doesn't know the real reason I agreed to this whole mess. I didn't say yes to being her fake husband because I wanted to rescue the beautiful woman from her family drama with a holiday marriage ruse. No, I agreed because of her father.

James Parker, CEO of Parker Ventures. One of the most elusive, high-profile clients I've been after for over a year now. He's old school, doesn't trust easily, and refuses to entertain cold calls or sit-down pitches. The kind of guy who'd only open his office doors if you were recommended by someone he trusted.

Or, I hope, if you are his daughter's brand-new husband.

I didn't plan on getting hitched in Vegas, though. I just meant to strike up a normal conversation with Lily at the bar—make a little small talk, drop a few names, maybe mention that I was looking to work with her father. But then she started talking about her family and how miserable she was about going home single for Christmas. And when she looked at me, with that glass of wine in her hand, a determined glint in her eye, and proposed... the universe handed me my way in. It was an opportunity I couldn't pass up.

Why not play along with her plan? A quick Vegas wedding, a few family-filled days in Snowflake Village, and before long, I'll win her father's trust. And once I was in his inner circle, the rest is easy.

But I can't tell Lily. She thinks this was some mistake brought on by too much wine and medication. She doesn't know of my plans to get close to her and start up a relationship. So, I keep my mouth shut and pretend I'm as confused as she is.

I glance over at her. She's staring out the window lost in thought. Probably dreading how this is going to go down when we show up at her family's place with a surprise husband in tow. I'd be lying if I said I wasn't curious about her, too.. All I really know is that she has an older sister— Jane, the perfect one. The one Lily was so worked up about at the bar. And her father, of course. The reason I'm here in the first place.

"I can feel you staring," Lily mutters, still looking out the window.

"I wasn't staring," I lie smoothly. "Just thinking about how great this is going to go."

She snorts. "Oh yeah, sure. I bet my parents will be thrilled when I introduce you as the stranger I accidentally married in Vegas."

"Come on, your mom will probably love me. I'm very charming," I say, throwing her a grin. She rolls her eyes, but the corner of her mouth twitches upward.

"What about my dad?" she asks after a beat, her voice a little more hesitant. "He's… um… not exactly easy to impress."

That's what I'm counting on. "Don't worry. Dads love me."

That gets a scoff out of her. "You must have some kind of magic, because I've never met anyone who can win him over."

"I'm full of surprises." More than you know, Lily.

Her dad may be tough to impress, but I've played the long game before. I did my research. I'm not like the other guys she's dated. I'll be the perfect husband—attentive, respectful, everything her father would want for his daughter. Once he sees how serious I am about "making this work" with Lily, he'll start to trust me. And when that happens, I win.

The SUV crunches over snow as Snowflake Village, the small, festive town, comes into view. The streets are lined with twinkling Christmas lights, shop windows covered in garland, and people bundled in scarves and coats are walking with steaming cups of coffee and hot cocoa. It's disgustingly charming, and I can't help but believe in holiday magic or whatever seeing the Christmas-card-perfect town.

"Home sweet home," Lily mutters.

"Looks like a Hallmark movie," I say, not even bothering to hide the amusement in my voice. "You really grew up here?"

"Yup," she says, staring straight ahead, voice flat. "Every gingerbread-flavored, tinsel-covered inch of it."

I chuckle, but internally, I'm doing the math. Two weeks here, tops. That's all it should take. I'll win over her dad, secure Parker Ventures as a client, and then, once the holiday festivities are over, Lily and I will quietly annul this whole thing. She'll probably be relieved. And me? I'll be on the fast track by landing one of the biggest deals of my career.

But until then, I have to play the part. Husband of the year. Completely committed to the role.

I park the car outside the Parker family cabin—a sprawling, picturesque lodge surrounded by snow-dusted evergreens—and turn to Lily with my best reassuring smile. "Ready to introduce your husband to the family?"

She groans, dropping her head into her hands. "I still can't believe I'm doing this."

"Hey, don't worry." I reach over and give her hand a light squeeze. "I've got your back."

And for the first time, I'm not even lying. I do have her back... at least until I get what I came for.

After that? Well, it'll be time to remind Lily that what happens in Vegas doesn't always stay in Vegas. Sometimes, it just gets annulled.

Chapter 4

Lily

It's showtime. The Parker family cabin looks exactly like it did the last time I was here—a gingerbread house come to life. Snow piles high against the logs, and the roof is dusted in white like powdered sugar. There's a huge wreath hanging on the front door, complete with an obnoxious red bow. Honestly, the place looks like it's straight out of a holiday commercial for hot cocoa. And normally, I'd be happy to see it.

But now? I'm about to introduce my husband—the man I married on a whim in Vegas—to my family. Without, you know, telling them about the whole "married in Vegas" thing.

Cole steps out of the car and stretches, looking completely unbothered by the fact that we're about to walk into my family's holiday celebration as newlyweds. His grin is effortless as he glances at me. "You're thinking about bolting, aren't you?"

"Thinking? I'm actively planning my escape route," I mutter, eyeing the thick trees that surround the cabin. Maybe I could just disappear into the woods and live with the squirrels.

He chuckles, crossing around the car to stand next to me. "You'll be fine. Besides, who wouldn't want to meet me? I'm a delight."

"You keep saying that, but I'm starting to think it's just a rumor you spread about yourself."

"Hey, rumors have to start somewhere." He winks, and I roll my eyes, but there's a small smile tugging at my lips. He's annoyingly charming. It's the only thing keeping me from completely freaking out right now.

As we walk up the stone path to the front door, my stomach knots tighter with each step. My dad isn't exactly Mr. Warm and Fuzzy. My mom, on the other hand, will love Cole, which is almost worse. She's the type to immediately start talking about grandkids.

I stop at the door, glancing at Cole. "Last chance to run for it."

He smirks. "Nah, I'm good. Besides, you need me. I'm going to help you survive this holiday."

"Bold of you to assume I can't survive it without you," I mutter under my breath, reaching for the doorknob.

Before I can knock, the door flies open, and there's my mom, arms outstretched, looking festive in a red turtleneck and snowflake earrings jingling. "Lily! You're here!"

I barely get a chance to step over the threshold before she's pulling me into a hug. "Hi, Mom."

"And who's this handsome man?" she asks, her eyes landing on Cole. Her smile widens. "You must be the husband Lily warned me about!"

I feel my face heat up. Of course, I sent my mom a text on the way and my mom is diving right in. No warm-up, no easing into the conversation—just straight to the point. I open my mouth to answer, but Cole beats me to it.

"That's me," Cole says smoothly, holding out a hand. "Cole Rivers. It's a pleasure to meet you, Mrs. Parker."

My mom's eyes light up as she shakes his hand. "Oh, please, call me Bonnie! None of that 'Mrs. Parker' business. We're family now!"

Oh God.

I glance over at Cole, fully expecting him to be thrown by her enthusiasm, but nope—he's smiling like this is all perfectly normal. "Bonnie it is, then. And can I just say, you've got a beautiful home."

I resist the urge to roll my eyes. Smooth. He's laying it on thick, and my mom's eating it up.

"Thank you!" She beams. "We're so happy to have you here for the holidays. Now come in, come in. Everyone's in the living room."

I follow her inside, Cole at my heels, and my brain is already running through potential escape routes again. What have I done? I can't believe I married a guy I barely know, and now I'm parading him in front of my family like this is normal. Starting my winter vacation in Vegas was the first terrible idea and now that terrible idea has snowballed into bringing Cole home.

We step into the living room, and my dad's sitting in his usual chair by the fireplace, the picture of holiday stoicism. He's nursing a scotch, telling me he's already on edge. Perfect. This is not going to go great.

"Dad," I say, plastering on a smile. "This is Cole."

My dad looks up, giving Cole a slow, measured once-over. Classic James Parker. "So, you're the man who married my daughter in Vegas."

I freeze. "Uh, right, so about that—"

"Yes, sir," Cole cuts in smoothly. "It was spontaneous. And the best decision I've ever made."

I blink, taken aback by his confidence. Cole stands there, cool as a cucumber, and I have to admit—he's selling this whole "perfect husband" thing better than I expected. My dad narrows his eyes, but after a tense pause, he grunts and nods.

"Well, let's hope you can handle her," my dad mutters, taking a sip of his scotch.

Cole grins, leaning down to whisper in my ear, "Guess he likes me."

I shoot him a look. "Don't get cocky."

My mom, meanwhile, claps her hands together. "Now that the introductions are done, let's get you two settled in. I've put you in the guest cabin out back—"

"Guest cabin?" I blink, glancing at Cole. "Wait, both of us?"

"Oh, of course. You're married," my mom says, waving a hand like it's the most obvious thing in the world. "It's only natural you'd want your own space. It's all decorated for Christmas, too—lights, wreaths, the whole nine yards!"

I open my mouth to protest, but Cole squeezes my hand, cutting me off. "That sounds perfect, Bonnie. Thanks so much."

I turn and glare at him. "Perfect?"

He leans down again, his voice low enough for only me to hear. "Relax. If we don't share a cabin, it's going to look suspicious."

I narrow my eyes. "You seem way too comfortable with this."

He grins. "I'm just trying to be the perfect husband."

"You're trying too hard."

"Maybe," he says with a wink, "but your mom loves me already. That's gotta count for something."

I bite my lip to keep from smiling. It's frustrating how effortlessly he's sliding into this role, like he's done it a hundred times before. Meanwhile, I'm still trying to wrap my head around the fact that this isn't some terrible dream.

"Fine," I mutter, crossing my arms. "But I swear, if you snore, you're sleeping in the car."

He chuckles. "Noted."

Just then, Jane walks in—my older sister, the epitome of holiday perfection in her cashmere red sweater dress and matching lipstick. She takes one look at me, then at Cole, and her perfectly manicured eyebrows shoot up.

"Well, well, well," Jane says, crossing her arms. "So this is the mystery man who swept my baby sister off her feet."

"Oh God," I mutter. "Here we go."

But Cole? He just smiles, holding out a hand. "Nice to meet you. Lily's told me a lot about you."

"Has she now?" Jane's eyes flick to me, amusement dancing in them. "All good things, I'm sure."

"All great things," Cole says smoothly, and I swear Jane actually blushes. Traitor.

I give him a sidelong glance. "You're too good at this."

He grins, his eyes sparkling with mischief. "I aim to please."

Great. Now I've got to survive not only my family holiday but also my fake husband who's a little too good at pretending.

I can't help but wonder how well he's going to be at pretending when we share the tiny cabin tonight.

Chapter 5

Cole

This place is... cozy.

The kind of cozy that screams "Christmas threw up all over me." There's garland strung across the ceiling beams, twinkling lights wrapped around every available surface, and I'm pretty sure that the snowman pillow on the bed is winking at me. There's a faint smell of pine and vanilla in the air—either from a candle or some kind of Christmas magic. I can't tell.

Lily, on the other hand, looks less than impressed. She drops her bag onto the floor with a thud and flops onto the bed with an exaggerated sigh. "This is ridiculous."

I stifle a smile. "What? You don't like the festive cabin charm? Look at all this holiday cheer."

She sits up, narrowing her eyes at me. "If by 'holiday cheer,' you mean 'overwhelming amount of tinsel,' then yes. It's fantastic."

I chuckle, pulling my suitcase toward the dresser and start to unpack. "You know, for someone who dragged me to a Christmas village, you're not exactly bursting with Christmas spirit."

She glares at me. "I didn't drag you here. You volunteered to come. Remember?"

"Right." I grin, tapping my ring and folding a sweater. "I'm here entirely of my own free will. No coercion involved whatsoever."

"Exactly," she says, and then pauses, looking confused. "Wait... was that sarcasm?"

"Who, me? Never."

She shoots me a look but doesn't say anything, which I take as a win. I continue unpacking, though my eyes keep drifting back to her as she sits cross-legged on the bed, sorting through her own clothes. It's hard not to notice how pretty she is, especially when she's scowling at me like I'm the cause of all her problems.

Her dark hair is a little messy from the long drive, and there's a natural flush to her cheeks from the cold outside. She's wearing this oversized sweater that falls off one shoulder, revealing smooth skin, and it's doing absolutely nothing to help me focus.

I look away, trying to distract myself by neatly arranging my shirts. This was supposed to be easy. Get close to her dad, land the deal, and move on. No complications. But of course, Lily herself is a complication. A very attractive, very stubborn complication.

"So," she says, breaking the silence, "how exactly are we supposed to pull this off?"

"Pull what off?" I ask, glancing at her.

She gives me a pointed look. "This. The whole married couple act. You do remember we've only known each other for, like, a day, right?"

"Oh, I remember," I say, leaning against the dresser with my arms crossed. "But your parents don't need to know that. As long as we don't contradict each other, we'll be fine. Just follow my lead."

"Follow your lead?" she snorts. "That sounds like a recipe for disaster."

"Hey, I'm a great leader."

"Sure you are, Captain Christmas," she says with an eye roll.

I grin. "Nice nickname. I'll wear it with pride."

She groans and flops back onto the bed. "This is a nightmare. I can't believe I'm in the middle of the mountains with a guy I married by accident. At least we're not actually sharing the bed."

I glance at the bed—huge, soft, and covered in Christmas-themed blankets. I can't help but imagine what it would be like if we *were* sharing it. Not that I'd ever say that out loud.

"Technically, we are married," I point out, unable to resist. "So sharing a bed wouldn't be that weird."

Lily shoots upright so fast she nearly topples off the bed. "Don't even think about it."

I laugh, raising my hands in surrender. "Relax, I'm kidding. I'll take the couch."

Her eyes narrow suspiciously. "You're awfully good at pretending to be all husbandly. Almost like you've done this before."

I shrug, unable to keep from smirking. "What can I say? I'm a fast learner."

"Great," she mutters, rubbing her temples. "Just what I need—Mr. Perfect Husband. My parents are going to love you."

"Thanks," I say, unpacking the last of my things. "I do have that effect on people."

"Ugh," she groans again, collapsing back onto the bed. "This week is going to be a nightmare, isn't it?"

I glance at her, taking in the way she's sprawled out across the comforter, her hair fanned out like she belongs in some holiday romcom poster. For a split second, I imagine what it'd be like if this wasn't just a deal for her dad's business. If we were actually here as newlyweds. If I could kiss her without thinking about my ulterior motives.

But no. I can't get distracted. This is all just part of the plan. She's just a means to an end.

"Could be worse," I say, trying to shake the thoughts out of my head. "At least you've got me to run holiday interference. It's not like I'm a jerk."

"Oh, I don't know," she says, peeking up at me with a sly grin. "The jury's still out on that."

I laugh, shaking my head. "You wound me, Lily."

She smirks. "You'll survive."

I look at her for a moment longer, and for some reason, I find myself looking forward to spending the holiday with her.Because the more time I spend with her, the less sure I am that I'm only doing this for a business deal.

Chapter 6

Lily

The next morning, we're all crammed into the little shops lining Snowflake Village, and I'm pretty sure I've hit my limit for festive holiday spirit. Jane, on the other hand, is in her element. She's gliding from store to store like some kind of Christmas fairy, perfectly put together in her designer coat and boots, while I feel like a lump in my oversized sweater and beanie.

Her husband, of course, is trailing behind her like the perfect doting spouse, carrying all her shopping bags with a smile. They're like an advertisement for happily-ever-after, and I'm the sad little footnote at the bottom of the page.

Except... I glance over at Cole, who's beside me, hands in his pockets, looking all sorts of handsome in his dark coat. His hair's a little ruffled from the cold wind, and there's this rugged, easygoing charm about him that just… works. Especially against the backdrop of twinkling lights and snow-dusted trees.

It hits me again—why would a guy like him agree to this? To me?

I tug my scarf a little tighter around my neck and shove the thought away. I don't need to be reminded of how completely bizarre this whole situation is. I married a stranger, and now I'm parading him around my hometown like a Christmas prize I scored during Black Friday.

"Lily, look!" Jane chirps, holding up yet another perfectly wrapped box of artisanal chocolates. "Wouldn't these be cute for stocking stuffers?"

I force a smile. "Adorable."

Jane's eyes flicker over to Cole, her smile growing even wider. "So, Cole, tell me—what's it like being married to my little sister? Is she as high maintenance as I remember?"

I open my mouth to respond, but Cole beats me to it. "She's a dream," he says smoothly, flashing one of those killer smiles. "No complaints from me."

My cheeks warm, not from the cold but from the way his words slide so effortlessly out of his mouth. He's good at this. A little *too* good. I don't even know why he agreed to this crazy plan, but he's playing the role of perfect husband like he's a master of deception.

Jane raises an eyebrow at me like she's impressed, but I can tell she's sizing him up. That's her way—always measuring, always comparing. And why wouldn't she? She's got her perfect life wrapped in a bow, and now I've suddenly shown up with *Mr. Handsome Perfect Businessman*.

"Yeah," I mumble, grabbing a random scarf from a rack. "A real dream."

Cole leans over, just enough that his breath brushes my ear, and says quietly, "That sounded convincing."

I elbow him, fighting the urge to smile. "Shut up."

He chuckles, but it's low enough that only I can hear it. There's something about his laugh—like it's meant just for me—that makes my stomach do a little flip. Great, now I'm noticing how attractive he is and how he smells faintly like pine and something warm and spicy. Like I needed more complications.

We manage to get through the rest of the shopping trip with Jane and her husband still casting occasional curious glances our way. By the time we're all done, I'm exhausted from pretending everything is normal. Cole, on the other hand, seems completely unfazed, strolling through the village like he's been doing this holiday family thing for years.

I don't get it. Why isn't he freaking out like I am?

Later that evening, we're all sitting in my parents' living room, gathered around the fire with mugs of hot chocolate. It's a cozy scene that belongs on the front of a Christmas card—if that Christmas card also came with a side of interrogation. Because now, with everyone settled in, my parents and Jane are turning their full attention on me and Cole.

"So," my mom says, leaning forward eagerly, her eyes practically sparkling. "Tell us more about your love story! How did you two meet? Was it love at first sight?"

Cole and I exchanged glances. The heat rises to my cheeks as I try remembering the script we haven't reviewed yet. How are we supposed to sell this when we barely know each other?

"Yeah, tell us the details," Jane adds, her eyes gleaming with that competitive edge she always gets when it comes to relationships. "I want to hear everything."

Cole's hand casually rests on my knee, and I have to bite down on my lip to keep from flinching. He's just acting, I remind myself. This is all for show.

"Well," Cole begins smoothly, flashing that easy grin that seems to come so naturally to him, "we met at a bar, actually. It was pretty unexpected."

That part, at least, is true.

I nod, trying to play along. "Yeah, um, I was just having a drink, thinking about the holidays, and then he... showed up."

"And swept her off her feet," Cole finishes, shooting me a wink. "She couldn't resist me."

I snort, despite myself. "More like I was distracted by the terrible bar music, and he caught me off guard."

Jane narrows her eyes suspiciously. "So, who made the first move?"

My brain short-circuits. Who did make the first move? Did I propose to him? What on earth was I thinking? But before I can panic, Cole jumps in again, saving the day.

"Oh, she definitely made the first move," he says with a smirk. "She's bold like that."

"Really?" My dad pipes up, clearly impressed. "That's my girl."

I nearly choke on my hot chocolate. "Yep, that's me. Bold."

Cole squeezes my knee gently, and I give him a side-eye. What is this? He's almost too good at this. My family is eating it up, nodding and grinning like this is the best holiday romcom they've ever seen. It's unnerving how easily he's pulling it off.

"So, when did you know?" my mom asks, her voice softening like she's about to hear the most romantic story of all time. "When did you know she was the one?"

I freeze, my breath catching. How am I supposed to answer that?

But Cole doesn't miss a beat. "Honestly? The moment I saw her. Something about her just felt… right." His voice is low, sincere, and for a second, I almost believe him. Almost.

I stare at him, wide-eyed, wondering how he's managing to weave this story so effortlessly. Is it possible he's got some ulterior motive? Because no normal person would be this calm while lying to an entire room of people.

"Aw," Jane coos, her smug expression softening just a little. "That's so sweet."

I take a sip of my hot chocolate to avoid having to respond, my mind swirling with questions I don't want to ask. Why did he agree to this? Why is he so willing to play along with this ridiculous charade? And, more importantly, why am I starting to care what he thinks?

Because for a guy who's supposed to be my fake husband, Cole Rivers is doing a hell of a job making it feel real. *Too real.*

Chapter 7

Cole

The wind whips through my hair as I push the sled down the hill, laughing as Jane's kids, Ella and Ben, scream with pure, unfiltered joy. I've been running up and down this hill with them for what feels like hours, but I'm not even close to tired. These kids have more energy than I expected, and apparently, so do I.

"Uncle Cole!" Ella yells, holding up her mittened hand for a high five as she tumbles off the sled at the bottom of the hill. I jog down to meet her, slapping her tiny hand, feeling a surprising sense of pride at how easily I've slipped into this family man role. "We're gonna beat Aunt Lily next time, right?"

"Absolutely," I say, giving her a conspiratorial grin. "I've got a secret weapon. You ready?"

She nods eagerly, eyes wide with excitement, while Ben bounces around beside her, shouting something about how Aunt Lily doesn't stand a chance. I glance back up the hill where Lily is standing with Jane and her husband, Matt, shaking her head with a smile that's part amusement, part exasperation.

I catch her eye and can't help but grin. She's wrapped up in her oversized puffer jacket and a knit hat, her cheeks rosy from the cold, and she looks... well, she looks adorable, if I'm being honest. There's something about seeing her like this—relaxed, laughing, surrounded by her family—that makes me momentarily forget why I'm really here.

"Cole!" Ben tugs on my jacket, snapping me out of my thoughts. "Come on! We gotta beat them!"

"On it, buddy," I say, pulling the sled back up the hill. Ella grabs one side, and Ben grabs the other, and the three of us trudge our way through the snow on a mission.

By the time we reach the top, Lily's already climbed into her sled with a competitive glint in her eyes. "You sure you're ready for this, Cole?" she calls out, a smirk tugging at her lips. "I was a sledding champion back in the day."

"Oh yeah?" I raise an eyebrow, adjusting my gloves. "Well, I've got two secret weapons here, so don't get too cocky."

Lily looks down at Ella and Ben, then back at me, her smirk widening. "They're no match for me. I've got years of experience."

"You've got a big mouth for someone about to lose," I shoot back, trying to hide how much I'm enjoying this.

The banter, the teasing—none of it feels forced. It feels… natural.

"Let's see what you've got, then," she says, turning to Jane and giving her a playful nudge. "Jane, you ready to witness your sister's victory?"

Jane rolls her eyes but laughs, shaking her head. "Honestly, I'm just here to watch the chaos."

"And chaos there will be," I mutter under my breath as Ben and Ella scramble into the sled with me. "Alright, you two. Hold on tight. We're going to show Aunt Lily how it's done."

The next few seconds are a blur of snow, wind, and shrieking laughter as we fly down the hill, narrowly avoiding bumps and trees. I can hear Lily laughing behind us, but she's not catching up. By the time we reach the bottom, Ella and Ben are cheering like they just won an Olympic gold medal.

"Victory!" Ella shouts, throwing her arms in the air. Ben's bouncing in the sled beside her, beaming with pride.

I glance over my shoulder to see Lily skidding to a stop, a mock scowl on her face as she dusts snow off her jacket. "Alright, alright," she says, her tone playful. "I'll admit defeat… this time."

I stand up, helping the kids out of the sled, and shoot Lily a smug grin. "Told you. You didn't stand a chance."

Lily narrows her eyes at me but there's warmth behind them. "I'll get you back. Just wait."

I step closer, lowering my voice so only she can hear. "I'm looking forward to it."

She blinks, caught off guard for a second, but then she smiles, shaking her head like she's still trying to figure me out. Honestly, I'm trying to figure myself out too. There's something about this—*about her*—that's throwing me off my game.

"Lily," Jane calls out from behind us, breaking the moment. "Can we talk for a sec?"

Lily nods, following Jane to the side while I stay with the kids, giving them a few pointers on sledding strategy—like I'm some expert or something. Out of the corner of my eye, I watch as Jane leans in to Lily, her voice low, but not so low I can't hear bits and pieces of their conversation.

"You know," Jane says, "I've always envied you, Lily."

Lily looks genuinely surprised. "You've envied me? You're kidding, right? You're perfect. You have everything."

Jane shrugs, a small smile on her face. "Yeah, but you're spontaneous. Adventurous. You always go after what you want without overthinking it. It's something I've never been able to do."

Lily glances back at me, her expression softening slightly. I wonder what's going through her mind. Does she regret all of this? Does she still think marrying me was some impulsive mistake?

Later that evening, after we've had dinner and the kids are settled, I finally spot my opportunity. Lily's dad, James, is sitting by the fireplace, nursing a glass of scotch. He's the whole reason I concocted this insane plan in the first place—the chance to win him over as a client. James Parker is a big deal in the business world, and if I can get him on my side, it'll open doors for me I wouldn't be able to open on my own.

But first, I have to get him to like me.

I casually make my way over to the fireplace, pretending like I'm just looking for a quiet moment to relax. Mr. Parker glances up as I approach, raising an eyebrow.

"Cole," he says, gesturing to the chair across from him. "Care to join me?"

Perfect. This is my chance.

"Don't mind if I do," I reply, sitting down and accepting the glass of scotch he pours for me. "Beautiful place you've got here. I can see why Lily loves coming home for the holidays."

James smiles, though it doesn't quite reach his eyes. "Yeah, she's always been attached to this town. Stubborn, like her mother."

I nod, taking a sip of the scotch and letting the warmth spread through me. "I admire that about her. She's got a strong sense of loyalty. It's one of the things that stood out to me when we met."

James looks at me for a long moment, like he's weighing my words, trying to figure me out. I hold his gaze, hoping I come off as sincere, as the kind of guy he'd want to do business with.

"Loyalty's important," James finally says, leaning back in his chair. "But so is honesty."

I nod, my heart thudding in my chest. "Absolutely."

James's eyes narrow slightly, and for a moment, I wonder if he's onto me. If he somehow knows this whole marriage is just a charade, that I'm only here to get closer to him. But then he nods, taking another sip of his scotch.

"Good," he says, his tone lighter now. "That's what I like to hear. Welcome to the family, Cole."

I relax slightly, relieved that I haven't blown it. Not yet, anyway.

Chapter 8

Lily

The next day dawns crisp and cold, the air biting but fresh as we drive toward Tinsel Christmas Tree Farm. Snowflakes twirl lazily from the gray sky, coating the world in white. I glance at Cole, who's sitting beside me in the driver's seat, one hand on the steering wheel, the other resting casually on his knee. There's something oddly comforting about him being here. Maybe it's the fact that we're doing something as simple as picking out a Christmas tree together. Like we're a real couple. A real husband and wife.

Stop it, Lily, I mentally scold myself. Remember what Jane said. She envies you for being spontaneous, for taking risks. It's time to start acting like that version of yourself again.

But, seriously—Jane envies me? I'm still floored by that revelation. My sister, with her perfect husband and perfect kids, looking at my messy life with any kind of admiration? It's like finding out reindeer actually fly.

Cole pulls into the farm parking lot, snapping me out of my thoughts. We step out of the car, and I pull my scarf tighter around my neck, trying to shield myself from the chill. The farm is lined with rows of pines and firs, each tree dusted with snow, waiting to be someone's holiday centerpiece. The smell of pine is intoxicating, and I inhale deeply, letting it fill my senses.

"You ready to find the perfect tree, Mrs. Rivers?" Cole asks with a grin, his breath coming out in little clouds.

"Lead the way, Mr. Rivers," I reply, trying to sound casual, though the way the word "Mrs." sounds next to his name still makes my stomach flutter.

We wander through the rows of trees, debating over which one is "the one." Cole, naturally, gravitates toward the taller, more imposing ones, while I insist on something cozier, a tree with a little more charm and character.

"You're seriously considering that one?" Cole asks, pointing at a squat little tree with lopsided branches. "I've seen houseplants with more dignity."

I swat his arm playfully. "It has character. A tree doesn't have to be perfect to be loved."

He smirks, raising an eyebrow. "Is that your philosophy on trees or husbands?"

I roll my eyes, trying to suppress a smile. "Both, apparently."

Before he can respond, a familiar voice calls out, "Well, if it isn't Lily Parker!"

I turn to see Red, the owner of the tree farm and my old classmate, walking toward us. Her bright red hair is vibrant against the snowy backdrop, and she's wrapped in a festive green scarf. Red is larger than life, both in personality and appearance, and seeing her is a blast from the past.

"Red!" I exclaim, grinning as she gives me a quick hug. "How've you been?"

"Busy, as usual," she replies, her green eyes twinkling. "The holidays are my crazy season. Everyone wants the perfect tree, and I'm here to deliver. And who's this?" She glances at Cole, giving him a once-over with an approving nod. "Your boyfriend?"

Oh boy. This is where things get tricky.

"This is Cole," I say, trying to sound nonchalant. "Cole, meet Red. She runs this place and was in my class back in high school."

"Nice to meet you," Cole says, extending a hand. Red takes it, her smile widening as she shakes it.

"Well, aren't you a lucky one, Cole," Red says, her voice teasing. "Lily's a bit of a wild card, but that's part of her charm, right?"

I force a laugh, though inside I'm still reeling from Jane's words yesterday. I've always thought of myself as the messy, impulsive one, while Jane was the golden child. But what if I've been seeing it all wrong?

Red continues chatting about the farm, the holiday rush, and her booming business. I nod along, but my mind is elsewhere, swirling with thoughts of what Jane said. How she envied me. The idea of it feels so foreign, like trying on someone else's coat and finding out it fits.

After a bit more catching up with Red, Cole and I return to our search for a tree. He wants one that's tall enough to require scaffolding to decorate, while I'm set on finding one with personality. Something that fits us, even though I'm not entirely sure what *us* even is.

We finally compromise on a mid-sized tree with thick, full branches and a sweet pine scent that hits you the moment you're near it. Its branches are poking out drunkenly—not perfect, but it's like us.

"See? This is the one," I say, crossing my arms with satisfaction as I gesture toward the tree.

Cole eyes it, then shrugs. "Alright, I'll admit—it's not bad. I can work with this."

We get the tree loaded up and pay for it, chatting lightly with Red as we make our way back to the car. Cole helps secure it to the roof of the car. Once we're back inside, he cranks the heater up to chase away the chill, and I can't help but steal a glance at him.

He's got that easy, confident way about him that makes me wonder why he agreed to any of my holiday drama. He could've easily said no. So why did he say yes?

"Hey, Cole," I start, my voice softer now. "I've been meaning to ask… why did you agree to this? Marrying me, I mean."

He turns to look at me, his expression unreadable. "Why wouldn't I?"

I blink, caught off guard by the question. "I don't know. It's just… I was a complete mess that night. I don't even remember half of it. And you—well, you could've walked away. But you didn't."

Cole's quiet for a second, then he shrugs, giving me a playful smile. "Maybe I just like a good adventure."

"Adventure?" I repeat, laughing despite myself. "You call this an adventure?"

"Absolutely," he says, his voice teasing but with a hint of something deeper. "And you, Lily Parker, are the most unpredictable part of it."

I shake my head, though my heart's doing that stupid little fluttering thing again. Maybe it's the way he's looking at me, or maybe it's the fact that, for the first time, I'm actually the main character in someone's story. Not just tagging along—he really sees me.

And then I think about Jane, about how she's always been the golden child—the one with the perfect life. But maybe my chaotic, impulsive way of doing things isn't so bad after all.

"Ready to head home, Mrs. Rivers?" Cole asks, turning the key in the ignition.

I glance at him, biting back a smile. "Let's do it, Mr. Rivers."

As we drive back to the house with the tree strapped to the roof, I lean my head against the window, watching the snow-covered trees whiz by. And for the first time, I don't feel like I'm competing with Jane, and trying to live up to some impossible standard.

I feel like I'm exactly where I'm supposed to be.

Even if I have no idea what's coming next.

Chapter 9

Cole

The moment we walk through the door with the Christmas tree, the smell of hot cocoa and gingerbread hits me like a warm hug. It's a stark contrast to the crisp winter air outside, and the living room is buzzing with holiday cheer as everyone gathers around. Lily's parents are laughing with Jane and her husband, the kids are running around in their Christmas pajamas, and everything feels…perfect.

Too perfect.

Lily grins up at me, her cheeks flushed from the cold, and for a second, I almost forget why I'm here. Almost. But then her dad walks over, clapping me on the back like we're old buddies, and reality comes rushing back.

"Got the tree, huh?" Mr. Parker says, his smile wide as he looks between us. "Good job, you two."

"Yeah, it's a beauty," I reply, trying to keep my voice light. I've got to play the part. Keep it cool. This whole charade hinges on me acting like *the* devoted husband, and so far, it's working. Maybe a little too well.

But then, Jane's voice cuts through the noise. "Oh my gosh! Look where they're standing!"

I follow her gaze up, and sure enough, there it is—a sprig of mistletoe hanging right above us. Just my luck. Lily looks up, her eyes widening before she lets out a nervous laugh.

"Oh, come on," Jane teases. "You have to kiss! It's tradition."

The whole room turns to watch us, and I can feel the anticipation in the air. There's no way out of this. I glance down at Lily, who's biting her lip, clearly just as nervous as I am. Then she meets my gaze, and something shifts. It's not awkward anymore. It's…electric.

"Well, Mrs. Rivers," I say, my voice low as I lean in a little, "looks like we've got to put on a show."

She rolls her eyes, but there's a sparkle in them that tells me she's not entirely against the idea. "When in Rome," she whispers, and before I can react, she closes the distance between us.

The kiss starts off slow, like we're testing the waters. But then, almost without warning, it deepens. I slide my hand around her waist, pulling her closer, and the feel of her against me, the warmth of her lips—it's more than I expected. It's not for show anymore. It's something else. Something real.

And for a split second, I believe it. I believe that maybe I could be falling for her.

The sound of clapping and cheering pulls us apart, and I force a grin as Lily laughs, her cheeks flushed with more than just the cold. The room erupts in good-natured teasing, but all I can think about is the way my heart's racing from her kiss.

What the hell am I doing?

After we've set the tree up and decorated it, the house quiets down. The kids are asleep, Jane and her husband have retreated to their room, and Lily and I head out to the guest cabin. It's small and cozy, with just enough space for a bed and a couch.

"Goodnight," I tell her, pulling a blanket from the couch.

"You're sleeping on the couch" she asks, already pulling off her scarf and tossing it onto the bed. "I mean, we are married. You don't have to sleep on the couch tonight, Cole."

Her voice is teasing, but there's something else beneath it —something that makes me pause for just a second. But then I shake my head. "I think we've done enough for one day," I say with a grin. "You get the bed. I'll survive."

She shrugs, climbing into the bed and pulling the covers up to her chin. "Suit yourself. But if you wake up with a stiff neck, don't say I didn't warn you."

I chuckle, settling down on the couch. I lie there, staring at the ceiling, the soft glow of the Christmas lights from outside filtering through the window.

"So," Lily says, breaking the silence. "You've heard plenty about my family. Tell me about yours."

I stiffen, not sure how to answer that. I've been trying to avoid this conversation, but it's inevitable. "There's not much to tell," I finally say. "My parents...they weren't exactly the warm and fuzzy type."

Lily props herself up on one elbow, watching me with curiosity. "What do you mean?"

I take a deep breath. I'm not used to talking about this. Not with anyone. But something about the way she's looking at me—genuine and open—makes me want to tell her the truth. At least about this part.

"They weren't around much," I admit. "My dad was always working, and my mom...well, let's just say she had other priorities. I was kind of left to figure things out on my own."

Lily's face softens. "That sounds...lonely."

I shrug, trying to play it off. "I got used to it. Besides, it made me pretty independent. I learned early on that I couldn't rely on anyone but myself."

She's quiet for a moment, and then she says softly, "I can't imagine that. Growing up like that, I mean. My family can be a lot, but they've always been there."

I nod, swallowing the knot in my throat. "Yeah, I noticed."

There's a long pause, and then Lily speaks again, her voice barely above a whisper. "I'm sorry, Cole. Everyone should have a loving home, especially for the holidays."

Her words hit me harder than I expected. I'm not used to people caring. Not like this. And the guilt—*God, the guilt*—

settles heavy in my chest. Because the truth is, I'm lying to her. I've been lying from the start. This whole marriage, this whole act—it's all about getting close to her father. And yet, here she is, opening up to me like I'm someone who deserves it.

"I don't talk about it much," I finally say, trying to keep my voice steady. "But it's okay. I've moved on."

Lily nods, though her eyes stay locked on mine, like she's trying to figure me out. "Well," she says after a long pause, "if it makes you feel any better, I think you turned out pretty great."

I chuckle, though the sound feels hollow. "Thanks. I guess we'll see about that."

She smiles, then lies back down, pulling the covers up again. "Goodnight, Cole."

"Goodnight, Lily."

I close my eyes, but sleep doesn't come easily. Instead, I lie there, staring at the ceiling, my mind spinning. I should be focused on the plan, on what I came here to do. But all I can think about is her. The way she laughed with her family today, the way she kissed me under the mistletoe, the way she's letting me in even though she doesn't know the truth.

And that kiss—damn it, that kiss.

I shouldn't care. This was supposed to be simple. Get close to her dad, secure the deal, and move on. But nothing about this feels simple anymore.

Because for the first time, I'm starting to wish being part of their big, happy family wasn't a lie.

Chapter 10

Lily

I can't stop thinking about his kiss.

It's ridiculous, really. One kiss under the mistletoe, and now my brain's short-circuiting like a Christmas light that's making the entire string short circuit. But there's no denying that the moment Cole's lips touched mine, something in me sparked. It was warm, electric, and a little too real for what's supposed to be a holiday game—a fake marriage.

I lie in bed replaying it in my head, until the sound of laughter and banging dishes from the kitchen interrupts my thoughts. It's gingerbread house time—a family tradition, where everything is more about who can build the most outrageous creation than any actual architectural skill. I toss on a sweater and head into the house from the cabin outside to find everyone gathered around the table, bowls of candy and icing spread out like we're prepping for battle.

Cole's already there, sitting at the far end of the table, grinning like he's ready to take on the world. My stomach does this weird little flip when he looks at me and says, "Thought you were going to sleep through the competition, Mrs. Rivers."

I roll my eyes, grabbing a chair next to him. "Please, like I'd miss watching you crash and burn while trying to build a gingerbread skyscraper."

"Skyscraper? Who said anything about a skyscraper?" He arches a brow, flashing me that grin that I'm starting to realize might be dangerous for my health. "I'm thinking more along the lines of a gingerbread castle. Complete with a blue candy moat."

"A moat? Very festive," I tease. "Nothing says 'Christmas cheer' like an edible fortress."

"I'm a man of vision, Lily. You should know that by now."

"And yet, you married me in a Vegas chapel." I grin back, feeling a flush creep up my neck as we exchange banter. It's easy with him. Too easy. And that's what's scaring me a little.

"Exactly," he says, leaning in just a fraction, lowering his voice so only I can hear. "A man of vision and spontaneity. You said it yourself."

There's something in the way he says it, the playful lilt to his voice, that makes my heart beat faster. Maybe Jane was right. Maybe I do have this spontaneous streak in me that I've never really embraced. Maybe that kiss wasn't just a fluke.

I shake my head, trying to focus on the task at hand. "Well, I don't know about you, but I'm going to build the most structurally sound gingerbread house this table has ever seen."

Cole smirks, grabbing a piece of gingerbread and slathering icing on it. "You're on, Mrs. Structural Engineer."

"Stop calling me that."

"Make me."

I elbow him playfully, but the laughter that bubbles up between us feels different—lighter, flirtier. I'm not sure when the dynamic shifted, but somewhere between last night's kiss and now, something changed. And I can't help but notice how much I'm enjoying it.

We spend the next hour immersed in gingerbread construction, throwing bits of candy at each other and competing over whose house will survive an "earthquake" —aka Cole's version of gently shaking the table every time I get my roof to stay up.

"You're such a cheater," I laugh, pressing a piece of gumdrop on the roof as it wobbles.

"Not cheating. It's called testing the integrity of your structure."

I narrow my eyes at him, but I can't help the smile tugging at my lips. "I'm watching you, Rivers."

"And I'm watching you, Mrs Rivers." He winks, and just like that, my heart does another one of those ridiculous flips.

By the time we finish, there's more candy on the floor than on the houses, and my masterpiece looks like something that's barely survived a gingerbread apocalypse. Cole, to his credit, manages to build an actual house with a turret and everything.

"Okay, I admit defeat," I say, holding up my hands. "You win."

"Of course I do," he says smugly, reaching over to tap a gingerbread chimney into place. "But yours has character."

"Thanks, I think?"

"Character's what counts, right?" He meets my eyes, and for a second, the air between us is charged. Like we're not just talking about gingerbread anymore. Like maybe, this whole thing has more character than I gave it credit for.

Before I can overthink it, my mom appears in the doorway, wiping her hands on a dish towel. "Lily, could I steal you for a second?"

"Uh, sure." I glance at Cole, who's busy trying to repair my disaster of a house, and follow her into the living room.

Mom sits down on the couch, patting the space beside her. I join her, suddenly feeling like I'm about to get one of her signature "talks."

"So," she starts, looking at me with that mom look—half amused, half knowing. "Cole seems like a really great guy."

I nod, trying to keep my face neutral. "Yeah, he's…he's great."

"You seem happier than usual with him."

I hesitate. "Do I?"

She gives me a soft smile, brushing a piece of hair behind my ear like she used to when I was a kid. "Lily, I know things have been hard for you lately. You've been trying to find your place and comparing yourself to your sister. But sweetheart, you don't need to compete with anyone. And honestly? I've never seen you this happy. Not in a long time."

I bite my lip, feeling a wave of emotions crash over me. It's true. I've always envied Jane. Her perfect life, her perfect husband, her perfect kids. But now… now I'm starting to realize that maybe there's more to happiness than what I thought. Maybe I don't need to be Jane. Maybe I can be myself and find my own version of happiness. And Cole… well, he's part of that.

"I guess I didn't realize how much I needed to be myself and find the right person," I admit softly.

Mom smiles, squeezing my hand. "Lily, you're wonderful. You deserve to be happy."

I nod, my chest feeling a little lighter. She's right. I do deserve this. Even if it's all a little messy and complicated, there's something here with Cole. Something real, or at least, something that could be.

And maybe it's time to stop questioning it and let myself believe in the possibility.

"Thanks, Mom," I say, leaning in for a quick hug.

She smiles again, but there's that glint of knowing in her eyes. "Now, go check on your husband before he eats all the gumdrops."

I laugh, heading back to the kitchen where Cole is, of course, sneakily stuffing his face with the leftover candy.

"Caught you," I tease, warmth spread through me as I enjoy the sight of him at ease with our little holiday traditions.

I realize that he probably doesn't have any family traditions to celebrate and my heart warms to see him happy. And just like that, I realize—I'm in trouble. Because I'm starting to develop feelings for my fake husband.

Chapter 11

Cole

It's snowing lightly when we pull up to the grand, festively lit lodge for the charity Christmas party. Twinkling lights drape across the roof and windows, and the faint sound of holiday music drifts out from the entrance as guests in their finest attire spill inside. This whole scene feels like a Christmas card come to life. But for once, I'm not focused on the charm of Snowflake Village or the picturesque surroundings.

I'm focused on Lily.

She's standing beside me in a dress that's making it hard to think straight. It's this deep emerald green, satin, flowing down to her ankles, with a neckline that's elegant but just low enough to drive me crazy. Her hair is pinned up in a messy bun with loose curls framing her face, and she looks like she belongs in some old Hollywood movie.

When she turns and smiles at me, I swear I forget to breathe for a second.

"Ready to charm the town, Mr. Rivers?" she teases, pulling her shawl tighter around her shoulders as we head inside.

If only she knew. I've been playing this whole thing like it's just a means to an end—a way to get closer to her father. But after last night's kiss, I'm starting to wonder if I'm getting played.

Because here's the truth I haven't wanted to admit: I like being her husband.

It hits me again as we step into the grand ballroom, where the town's upper crust is mingling. Lily takes my arm, and we move through the room, greeting people, shaking hands, and exchanging pleasantries. And every time she introduces me as her husband, I swell with pride.

"Everyone, this is my husband, Cole."

My husband, Cole. The words roll off her tongue like they've always belonged there. Like I belong there.

It's not part of the plan, not in the slightest, but when she says it, I wonder if this whole charade will become real. I can't stop glancing at her, catching the way she laughs easily with the townspeople, her eyes sparkling under the crystal chandelier's soft glow. I tell myself that I'm still playing, still pretending to be the devoted husband for her sake, to make her family holidays easier. But the truth? I'm starting to want this for me, too.

"Excuse me, darling," Lily says with a grin, slipping her hand into mine and leading me toward a group of her parents' friends. "I want you to meet a few people."

And I follow her, as if it's the most natural thing in the world.

We mingle for a while, making small talk, and I realize how good Lily is at this. She's warm, gracious, and confident, seamlessly navigating conversations. Watching her, I'm impressed—no, more than impressed—I'm in awe of how effortlessly she handles herself, especially with her family's expectations. And the longer I stand next to her, the harder it becomes to keep pretending .

Stepping away from the crowd for a breather, she catches my eye, tilting her head toward the dance floor. "Want to dance, Mr. Rivers?"

I genuinely smile, holding out my hand. "I thought you'd never ask."

We make our way to the dance floor, as the band starts up a slow, jazzy rendition of *The Christmas Song*. I pull her into my arms, and she rests her hand on my shoulder, her other hand slipping into mine.

I can't help but think about how perfectly she fits against me. How comfortable it feels, holding her like this.

"You look stunning tonight," I say, my voice low, almost more for me than for her.

She raises an eyebrow, but there's a playful glint in her eyes. "Oh? Is that part of the 'good husband' routine?"

I chuckle, shaking my head. "No. That's all me."

Her smile softens, and for a moment, we just sway together, the music wrapping around us like a Christmas quilt. It's peaceful, but there's an undercurrent of something deeper building between us. I don't know if it's the way she's looking up at me, or the way her fingers tighten slightly in mine, but it's like the whole world fades away, and all that's left is her.

I've spent so much time trying to convince myself that this was a means to an end. That Lily was just my way to get to her father. But right now? I don't care about business or clients or strategies. All I care about is her, in my arms, looking at me like I'm something more than just the guy she drunkenly married in Vegas.

"Do you always sweep women off their feet like this?" she asks, breaking the silence, though her tone is teasing.

"Only the ones who propose to me in Vegas."

She laughs, the sound light and musical, and it does something to me. Something I didn't expect. I find myself wanting more of it. More of her.

The music slows to an end, but neither of us moves. I keep my hand on the small of her back, holding her close, and she doesn't pull away. There's a moment—*a beat*—where I wonder if I should kiss her again. But before I can act on the impulse, the crowd around us begins to applaud, signaling the end of the song, and we reluctantly step apart.

As we make our way back to the family table, I feel this weird mix of emotions swirling inside me. Wanting her, yes, but also knowing I have to keep up the pretense. I can't let her know why I really agreed to this marriage in the first place. It would ruin everything. But damn it, it's getting harder and harder to keep the truth from her when all I want to do is be the guy she thinks I am.

The guy who's proud to be called her husband.

Later, after another round of mingling and a few too many holiday desserts, we head outside to where a roaring bonfire is crackling under the starry night sky. Lily's parents are chatting with some neighbors, and I spot her dad standing off to the side with a glass of eggnog. This is my chance.

"I'm going to grab a drink," I tell Lily, nodding toward the makeshift bar set up by the fire pit. "Want anything?"

"I'm good," she says, rubbing her hands together for warmth. "But hurry back."

I give her a nod, forcing myself to walk away before I decide to stay glued to her side all night. As I approach her dad, I take a deep breath, mentally preparing myself. This is what I came here for, after all—to build a connection with him, to secure his business. I just didn't expect Lily to get under my skin in the process.

"Mr. Parker," I say, stepping up beside him.

He turns, a slight smile tugging at the corner of his mouth. "Cole, my boy. Enjoying the party?"

"Yes, sir. It's been a fantastic evening."

We make small talk for a bit, but in the back of my mind, all I can think about is Lily. About how she's starting to make me want things I didn't know I wanted.

But for now, I keep my focus on the man in front of me. I can't let my feelings for Lily screw this up. Despite my plan, I somehow never get around to asking about a business partnership.

It's getting harder and harder to remember what my original plan was.

Chapter 12

Lily

With the charity party in full swing, I'm floating on a cloud of festive cheer. Everywhere I look, the warmth of the holiday spirit lights me up and everyone wants to congratulate me and talk to me. My family is laughing, friends are dancing, and the sweet scent of champagne and pine fills the air.

And then there's Cole. He's effortlessly charming everyone, blending into this world like he's always been part of it. I watch him from across the room, sharing a joke with my father, his smile wide and genuine. It makes my heart race in a way that's both thrilling and terrifying.

I can't deny it anymore: I'm falling for him.

The thought sends butterflies fluttering in my stomach. I never dive into relationships quickly, but with Cole, everything feels different. I want to take the leap and ask him about not getting an annulment and trying out marriage for real. What if he doesn't feel the same? What if this was all a fun charade for him?

"Hey, sis!" Jane suddenly appears beside me, a glimmer of mischief in her eyes. "You look like you're lost in thought. Is it about the handsome *Mr. Rivers?*"

I can't help but smile at my sister, even as a blush creeps up my cheeks. "Maybe a little. He's just... great, you know?"

Jane tilts her head, her gaze turning thoughtful. "He seems to make you happy."

"I am happy." Suddenly, all the pieces click into place. I want this. "I want the perfect life, like you have," I tell my sister.

She smiles. "It isn't always perfect, ya know? Sometimes you have to work hard for it."

"Your life is *super* perfect," I tease, nudging her playfully. "I mean, who else could pull off a sweater vest like your husband?"

She laughs, her eyes sparkling. "Point taken. But I see how you two are together. There's a connection. I think it's wonderful."

Before I can respond, I spot Cole across the room, chatting animatedly with another couple. I can't help but watch him; there's something magnetic about him. I'm so caught up in my thoughts that I barely notice Jane waving goodbye as she heads out to find her husband and kids.

Buoyed by our conversation, I excuse myself from the crowd and make my way to the bar for another eggnog.

The lively chatter swirls around me as I weave through the guests, feeling light and carefree.

I chat to a neighbor, and when I finish, I scan the ballroom. I can't find Cole anywhere.

Did he leave?

I wander over to find him, and turning a corner, I spot him hidden in a small alcove. He's on the phone, and I try not to eavesdrop, but it's kind of hard not to.

I freeze in my tracks when I hear him say my name. Who is he on the phone with? His aloof parents? But as I inch closer, his voice is too business-like for a personal call.

"Yeah, I'm getting closer to Mr. Parker," he says, his tone professional but still laced with that unmistakable charm. "Once I get him to sign on as a client, it'll be a huge win for the firm."

My heart sinks. Icy water douses all my earlier warmth. I hadn't considered that his interest in me could be tied to his career aspirations and my successful father.

I lean in, unable to resist. "I'll keep working on building a rapport with him," he continues. "I just need to keep playing the husband role a little longer. It's a winning strategy."

I feel like the wind has been knocked out of me. Everything we've shared—the laughter, the kisses, the moments that felt so intimate—was part of a plan to win my father?

As my heart begins to race with a mix of confusion and hurt, Cole suddenly turns. Our eyes lock, and my breath hitches as the realization flashes in his eyes. He knows I know.

It's eerily silent on the alcove. The laughter and music from the party blur into background noise, and all I can focus on is the flicker of surprise in his eyes—and the undeniable tension hanging between us.

I'm a raw nerve laid bare. What do I do now? What do I say? I'm left standing there, waiting for him to speak, my heart pounding as the impending storm gathers.

"This was all a scheme?" I choke out, my eyes widening.

"I can explain…" Cole reaches out, his words falling away.

I realize that I no longer care about anything he has to say. I have to get out of here. I turn around and flee, my feet running away from Cole as fast as I can.

I can't believe this. I can't believe I fell in love with the man who I thought was doing me a favor by playing my husband for my family holiday, but instead I was the one played! I've fallen in love with him and he's just following some sort of master plan.

I'm a fool, I think to myself as tears rush down my cheeks.

Chapter 13

Cole

I stand frozen, staring at Lily's wide eyes. Her face is a mix of shock and hurt. I can almost see her heart breaking, crumbling like a fragile piece of glass. I open my mouth to say something—*anything*—but the words stick in my throat.

The party swirls around us, oblivious to the bomb that just detonated. I take a step toward her, but she's already turning, disappearing into the crowd before I can explain.

Dammit.

I'm in motion before I even realize it, weaving through the clusters of people, searching for her. I keep replaying the look on her face, the exact moment she overheard me. Stupid. I was careless.

I should've never taken that call at the party. I was talking to a work colleague about our soon to be major client—

Lily's father—and now it looks exactly like what I feared it would. That I'm only with her for business. That all of this, her, us... is just some elaborate scheme.

I try to spot her auburn hair or the shimmer of her green dress through the crowd, but Lily is nowhere to be found. My chest tightens. I need to explain. I need to make her understand that she's more than a part of my business plan to me.

As I search, I feel eyes on me. Her family, her friends—they're all blissfully unaware of what just happened, but somehow, I can feel their judgment. Or maybe it's just my own guilt weighing heavy on my shoulders.

After a few frustrating minutes of searching, I accept that she's left the party. She's gone. I rub a hand over my face, trying to think clearly. I need to find her. But instead, I find someone else.

Mr. Parker. Her father.

He's standing near the fireplace, chatting with an older couple. I know now isn't the time, but the way my stomach twists with the weight of this mess, I don't see any other option. If I can at least make things right with him, maybe I can start fixing this whole situation. It's a long shot, but it's the only one I've got right now.

I make my way over, forcing a smile that feels about as authentic as a counterfeit bill. "Mr. Parker," I say, trying to sound casual, but the nerves in my voice betray me. "Mind if I steal you away for a moment?"

He turns, giving me a calculating look that makes it clear he didn't get to where he is by being easily impressed. He's a powerful man, and it's impossible not to feel a little intimidated under his gaze, even when I know this was the plan. The whole damn reason I'm here.

But right now, as I stand in front of him, none of that feels good. Not anymore.

"Cole," he says, his business demeanor changing into a smile as if I'm a real part of the family. "Of course, son. What can I do for you?"

That word—*son*—cuts right through me. I glance around, making sure no one else is within earshot. This is my chance. But the words aren't coming out like I planned. My mind is still reeling from Lily.

"I just wanted to thank you," I start, swallowing hard, "for the hospitality. I've been really enjoying spending time with your family."

"Likewise." His eyes crinkle with warmth, completely oblivious to the chaos going on in my head. "Lily's a great girl, isn't she?"

My stomach churns. I nod, my voice tight. "Yeah... she is."

I feel like a fraud. Here I am, standing in front of the man I came here to impress, all while the woman I'm starting to care about is probably somewhere wondering what kind of jerk she married.

"I'm glad to hear that," he says, clasping my shoulder. "Family is everything, Cole. That's what we live by. It's important to be with someone you can trust, especially when times get tough."

His words hit a little too close to home. I nod along, trying to swallow the guilt, but it's there, gnawing at me. I can't stop thinking about Lily and how she must've felt hearing that conversation. How she must think I'm nothing but a liar.

"You know, I've been keeping an eye on you two," he continues, oblivious to my inner turmoil. "You are good for each other. I can tell you really care about her."

I force another smile. "I do care about her," I say, and it's not a lie. Not anymore.

And that's what makes this all so complicated. What started as a calculated plan to get close to her father has turned into something I never saw coming. I didn't plan on falling for Lily. I didn't plan on wanting more than just a business connection.

I glance around the room again, hoping she'll magically appear, so I can explain everything. But she's nowhere to be found.

"Mr. Parker," I say, turning back to him, "I'd like to talk to you sometime soon about business. I think we could really work well together."

His smile widens, and he nods slowly, but I can tell his focus isn't really on business right now. "Of course, Cole. But let's save that for after the holidays. Right now, it's about family. Enjoy this time with Lily."

Family. That word again. I'm not sure I've ever felt further from it. But I'm starting to understand what the word means now.

I force another smile, but inside, I know I'm losing her. And the worst part? I don't blame her. If I were in her shoes, I'd run too.

Chapter 14

Lily

Throwing another sweater into my suitcase, I barely notice how the neat stack is turning into a wrinkled mess. Not that it matters. My life is a worse mess right now, so it's fitting. I pause, hands gripping the fabric, my eyes burning with unshed tears. I was so stupid. So damn stupid.

How could I have fallen for him?

Cole Rivers. The charming, handsome guy who swooped into my life at just the right time. The guy who smiled at me like I was the only person in the room. The guy who kissed me under the mistletoe like he meant it. The guy who, apparently, only married me to get closer to my dad.

I swallow the lump in my throat, trying to keep it together, but it's no use. I'm back in my childhood bedroom, packing up my life like I'm some teenage girl running away from heartbreak, except this time, I'm not running. I'm retreating. Hiding.

I wipe a stray tear off my cheek, shaking my head at myself. How did I let it get this far? I knew something was off, didn't I? I mean, come on—I marry a guy I don't know, bring him home for the holidays, and actually start to believe it could work? Like some kind of freaking Hallmark movie. Of course, he wasn't in love with me. Of course, it was all part of some ridiculous plan.

I was just too desperate to see it.

A knock on the door pulls me out of my negative spiral, and I groan inwardly. "Come in."

The door creaks open, and Jane steps inside, her *perfect* blonde hair framing her *perfect* face in that *perfect* way. Of course, it's Jane—Miss Has-Her-Life-Together coming to check on me. The last person I want to see right now. Well, second-to-last. I definitely don't want to see *him*. My husband.

"What do you want?" I mutter, shoving another sweater into my suitcase, probably stretching the zipper beyond repair.

"I heard you were packing," Jane says softly, stepping into the room. "Mom said you're leaving."

"Yep. Gotta get back to my messy, non-perfect life," I say, barely glancing at her. "And, you know, run far away from my lying, non-perfect husband."

Jane doesn't say anything for a second, which is surprising. Usually, she's the first to offer her unsolicited wisdom. When she finally does speak, her voice is soft, like she's picking her words carefully. "Lily, you don't have to do this."

I snort. "Do what, Jane? Run? Or be the fool who fell for a guy who didn't actually want her?"

"Lily..." she starts, sitting on the edge of my bed, her fingers tracing the hem of my comforter. "I've always envied you."

I blink, thrown completely off guard. "What?"

She looks at me, her usually confident blue eyes looking vulnerable, raw. "You heard me. I've always envied you. Your spontaneity, your ability to just... go after what you want. You've always been so brave."

I let out a bitter laugh. "Yeah, well, look where that bravery got me. Married to a liar."

Jane sighs, reaching over to take my hand. "I know it doesn't seem like it now, but maybe it's not as black and white as you think."

"Really? Because it seems pretty clear to me. He married me because he wants Dad as a client. I overheard him talking about it at the party tonight."

Jane doesn't flinch. She just squeezes my hand tighter. "Lily, have you talked to him about it? Or are you running before you get any answers?"

I open my mouth to snap back, to say something biting, but I can't. Because she's right. I haven't talked to him. I've been packing and avoiding and stewing in my anger without giving him a chance to explain. Not that there's really an explanation that would make this better.

"I... I just don't know if I can handle hearing whatever lame excuse he comes up with," I admit, my voice breaking. "I actually thought he might care about me, Jane."

Jane's expression softens, and for the first time, I don't feel like she's the perfect older sister looking down at me. She just looks... sad. "Maybe he does care, Lil. You're the only one who can decide if this is worth fighting for."

I want to say something—*anything*—to deny it. But deep down, I know she's right. I'm scared. I'm terrified of being hurt again, of being used, but there's a tiny part of me that still wants to believe Cole might actually feel something real.

Before I can reply, there's another knock on the door. This time, it's Mom poking her head in.

"Lily, honey... you might want to come downstairs."

"What now?" I groan, wiping my face and straightening up, trying to appear somewhat composed.

She gives me a small smile. "Just... come."

I follow Mom and Jane down the stairs, my heart pounding. I don't know what I expect, but when I step into the living room, I freeze.

There, standing in the middle of the room, is Cole.

And he's holding a sign. A giant, glitter-covered sign that says, *I'm an idiot, but I love you.*

My heart stutters.

The room is silent, my entire family watching as Cole looks at me with this raw, vulnerable expression on his face. "Lily," he says, his voice hoarse. "I messed up. Big time.

But I swear, I never planned on hurting you, especially once I fell in love with you."

My breath catches in my throat. Did he just admit to loving me?

"I wanted to get closer to your dad," he continues, stepping closer, his eyes locked on mine. "But somewhere along the way... I fell for you. For your laugh, your stubbornness, the way you throw yourself into things without thinking twice."

Tears prick at my eyes, and I hate that I'm getting emotional. But it's impossible not to. Because here he is, putting it all out there in front of my family.

"I don't care about your dad's business anymore," he says, his voice low. "I just care about you. And if you give me another chance, I swear I'll spend every day proving that."

I blink back tears, my heart thudding painfully in my chest. I don't know what to say. Part of me is still angry. Part of me is still hurt. But another part of me—the part that's always been spontaneous, as Jane says—wants to run to him. Wants to believe that this could actually work.

So, instead of thinking, I do what I always do.

I act.

I cross the room, closing the distance, and before I can stop myself, I kiss him.

And this time, it feels real.

All of it.

Chapter 15

Cole

The second Lily's lips touch mine, relief washes over me so fast it almost knocks me off my feet. She's kissing me. I don't know how it happened, how I went from standing here, holding a ridiculous glitter-covered sign in front of her entire family–thanks to Ella and Ben's crafting glitter help–to having her back in my arms. I'm not questioning it. I'm just holding on for dear life, praying she doesn't pull away.

The sound of cheering registers somewhere in the back of my mind, but I barely process it. All I can think about is how soft her lips feel, how I can taste the salt of her tears on mine. This kiss feels different. It's not for show, not for the benefit of anyone watching. It's just for us. Just real.

When we finally break apart, I look down at her, searching her face for any sign of hesitation. But she's smiling—

small, tentative, but real. Her eyes are glassy, the anger is gone, replaced by something warm and hopeful.

I let out a shaky breath, still half-expecting her to change her mind, but instead, she stays close, her hand sliding into mine. "Cole..." she starts softly, her voice so low only I can hear. "I still don't know if I can trust you completely."

I nod, my throat tightening. "I know. I'm going to spend the rest of my life making it up to you, if you'll let me."

She squeezes my hand, and that small act feels like the biggest gift in the world. It's not complete forgiveness, but it's a start. I'll take it.

"Alright, lovebirds, give the rest of us a break," Jane teases, breaking the tension in the room.

I glance around the room, realizing her whole family is watching with huge grins. Her mom is dabbing at her eyes, and even Jane's husband looks teary eyed. This isn't just a win for me and Lily—it's a win for her... our whole family, too. They want this to work. They want me to be the guy to make Lily happy.

And God, I want to be that guy more than anything.

Her father steps forward, clearing his throat, and my pulse jumps. Out of all the people in this room, he's the one I'm most worried about. Not just because of the business deal, but because I know how much he means to Lily. Winning him over means more now than it ever did.

"Cole," he says, his deep voice cutting through the lingering cheers. His eyes are sharp, assessing me, but there's something else there now, too. Maybe respect? "I appreciate the grand gesture. But if you want to stay in my daughter's life, you'll have to prove that this isn't just a one-time show. You'll have to be all in."

I straighten, meeting his gaze head-on. "I know, sir. And I am. All in. For her."

His eyes narrow slightly, as if testing me, but then he nods, clapping a hand on my shoulder. "Good. That's what I like to hear."

Relief surges through me again, and I exhale slowly. I've still got a long way to go before I've earned their full trust —before I've earned Lily's trust—but I'll take this first step. I'll take it and run with it, doing everything I can to make sure I don't screw this up again.

Because I'm not just doing this for a business deal anymore. That part of me, the part that came into this whole situation with selfish motives, has been replaced by something I didn't see coming. I want to be with Lily. Really be with her.

As everyone starts milling around again, talking and laughing like normal, I pull Lily aside, my hand still holding hers tightly. She looks up at me, her eyes searching mine, and thank goodness, I see the flicker of that spark that ignited the first time we kissed.

"I'm sorry," I whisper, brushing a strand of her hair behind her ear. "I know I messed up, but I want you to know—this is real for me. You're real for me."

She bites her lip, her eyes softening. "I want to believe you, Cole. I just... need time."

"You can take all the time you need," I promise. "I'm not going anywhere."

She stares at me for a moment, then nods. "Okay."

It's a small word, but it's enough. It's a start.

Later, as we help decorate the tree with her family, laughing and sipping hot chocolate by the fire, I realize something I never expected when I walked into this crazy, impulsive marriage with Lily.

I would do anything for her.

The thought hits me like a ton of bricks. This was never supposed to happen. I wasn't supposed to fall for her. But now, standing here with her in my arms, surrounded by her family, I know it's too late.

I'm hers. Completely.

Epilogue

Lily

It takes about a week—no, maybe five days—for me to start trusting Cole again. It's funny how quickly things can shift when you stop overthinking them and just let yourself feel. I was ready to run, to go back to my messy, predictable life, but then Cole did something I didn't see coming.

He turned my dad down.

That's right. When Dad offered him the business deal he had been after, the thing that started this whole crazy marriage, Cole said no.

I watched it unfold, standing in the kitchen with my heart in my throat. My dad gave him the green light, basically a golden ticket, and Cole thanked him—genuinely—but said he didn't want to mix business with family. He wanted to earn my dad's respect, not buy it.

And I believed him. Really believed him.

So, fast-forward six months, and here we are. It's the Fourth of July, and we're back in Snowflake Village for the holiday. The air smells like barbecue and fireworks, and the entire town is gathered in the square, like some kind of festive postcard come to life.

I look around at the string lights hanging above us, the red, white, and blue banners fluttering in the warm breeze, and I feel this overwhelming sense of calm. Like for the first time, everything is exactly where it's supposed to be. Including me.

I'm leaning against the picnic table, watching Cole a few feet away, talking to my dad and laughing like they're old friends. It's surreal how different things feel now. There's no tension, no worry that Cole's got some ulterior motive. He's just... here. With me. And the best part is, I know that's all he wants to be.

"Can't believe he turned Dad down," Jane says, sliding up next to me with a grin. She's holding a soda, looking relaxed in her sundress, and I smile.

"I know. I almost passed out when it happened," I admit, glancing at her. "But it made me realize he's serious. Like, really serious."

Jane nudges me playfully. "So... are you two serious?"

I can't help the grin that spreads across my face. "I think so."

She raises an eyebrow. "You think so?"

"Okay, fine. Yes. We're serious."

"Good. Because I'm tired of Mom asking me for the next grandkid!" she teases.

I shake my head, speechless.

"I like this version of you. Happy Lily looks good in red, white, and blue."

I laugh, shaking my head as I glance at Cole again. His head turns just in time to catch my eye, and he flashes me this smile that still makes my heart flip, like we're back in Vegas, like I'm seeing him for the first time.

"You look good too," I say softly, turning back to Jane. "Happy Jane is kind of my favorite."

She bumps my shoulder, and I know we've come a long way. The envy I used to feel for her "perfect" life is gone, replaced by something better—an understanding that maybe we're both a little envious of each other. But that's okay. We've both got good things going for us now, and that's all that matters.

"Hey!" Cole's voice pulls me from my thoughts, and I look up to see him walking over, a bottle of lemonade in hand. He hands it to me with a wink. "You looked thirsty."

I take it, grinning. "So thoughtful."

He shrugs. "I try."

"Are you two done being adorable, or is this gonna go on all night?" Jane teases, but there's a softness in her tone. She's genuinely happy for me—for us.

I lean into Cole, who wraps his arm around my waist, pulling me closer. "Sorry, Jane. No promises."

The sky starts to darken, and soon enough, the fireworks begin, lighting up the night with bursts of color and sound. I watch them explode overhead, feeling Cole's warmth beside me, his hand resting on my hip like it's the most natural thing in the world.

"Happy?" he asks, his voice low in my ear, and I tilt my head up to look at him. He's not watching the fireworks. He's watching me.

"Very," I reply, meaning every word.

"Good," he says, leaning down to press a kiss to the top of my head. "Because I'm pretty sure I'll spend the rest of my life trying to make you even happier."

I smile up at him, the fireworks reflecting in his eyes. "Careful, Rivers. I might hold you to that."

"I'm counting on it, Lily."

As the fireworks crackle and pop above us, I realize something I never thought I'd feel again—contentment. Cole and I started out all wrong, but somewhere along the way, we found something real. Something worth fighting for.

He whispers something I've dreamed about but never told him: "Lily, will you marry me?"

I laugh.

"What I mean is, will you remarry me, here at the lodge in Snowflake Village for our anniversary? I want to give you an unforgettable party and a wedding that you won't forget this time. Your dad gave me his consent to marry you, *again*, and host the wedding. What do you say Mrs Rivers? Do you want to try it again but not in Vegas this time?"

I cry and say, "Yes." And I know, without a doubt, that I'm exactly where I'm meant to be, with who I'm meant to be with.

With Cole.

For always.

THE END

Thank you so much for reading A Husband For Christmas! Hope you loved Cole and Lily as much as I loved creating them!

Want more of Cole and Lily? Read all about their fabulous real wedding, and honeymoon!! CLICK HERE to read!

Want Red's story? From Tinsel Christmas Farms?

Red Tinsel is on a mission to save the beloved Tinsel Christmas Tree Farm, a winter wonderland that's been in her family for generations. Since her father's passing, both the farm and the town have been struggling, and she's determined to turn things around. But there's a Grinch in the mix—Mayfair Continental, the corporate giant with plans to bulldoze the farm and replace it with a soulless shopping center.

Enter Nick Wolf, *The Big Bad Wolf,* the ambitious city slicker from Chicago. He's determined to secure a promotion by sealing the deal for Mayfair Continental. His task? Convince Red to sell her family farm. Simple, right? He plans to charm his way through this, close the deal, and be back in the Windy City before you can say "Merry Christmas."

But Nick quickly learns that Red is no pushover. She meets his every proposal with fierce resistance, and sparks fly—both the infuriating and the flirtatious kind. Despite their clashing agendas, there's an undeniable attraction between them, and Nick starts to see that the farm isn't just land; it's Red's heart and soul.

As Christmas approaches, Nick finds himself torn between his career aspirations and the unexpected warmth of small-town life—and one particularly spirited woman. Will he sacrifice Red's dreams for his own, or will the magic of the holiday season melt his heart and lead him to a different kind of success?

CLICK HERE to read now!!

If you loved Cole and Lily's story in *A Husband For Christmas*, then you'll love Wyatt and Tori's story in *If Kisses Were Snowflakes*.

CHECK IT OUT HERE!

Find all the books in the Mistletoe Kisses Series at:

MISTLETOE KISSES FULL SERIES

About the Author

Em Tate is an author of sweet romances that leave you feeling good after each read. When she's not writing you can find her in her garden tending to all her favorite tulips and daffodils. She's been an avid reader since she was little, and she enjoys bringing her stories to life.

Sign up for her newsletter to stay up-to-date on her upcoming releases. CLICK HERE!!

Head over to Facebook to join Em Tate's Amazing Readers!! CLICK HERE to join for fun, exclusive give-aways, and so much more!!!

Also by Em Tate

This book is a part of the "Mistletoe Kisses" series, a collection of 38 heartwarming clean romance stories that will make your spirits bright. Featuring popular tropes such as Fake Dating, friends to lovers, grumpy sunshine, accidental marriages, cowboys, Christmas magic, and so much more! These tales of holiday romance will warm your heart and kindle your belief in Christmas magic. "Mistletoe Kisses" - Where one kiss can change everything.

Snowed in For Christmas Series

SNOWED IN WITH GRUMPY

SNOWED IN WITH GROUCHY

SNOWED IN WITH GRINCHY

Snowflake Village Christmas Series

SNOWFLAKES AND SECOND CHANCES

TINSEL AND TWIRLS

MISTLETOE AND MAGIC WISHES

SLEIGH BELLS AND SWEETHEARTS

PEPPERMINT AND CANDY CANES

Coming Soon

MY GRUMPY BOSS VALENTINE

Made in the USA
Columbia, SC
14 March 2025